Hawai'i's OCEAN ANIMALS Coloring and Activity BOOK

illustrated by

Hollyanne Shell

ISBN-13: 978-1-949000-00-9

First Printing, July 2018
Second Printing, November 2019
Third Printing, September 2021

BeachHouse Publishing, LLC
PO Box 5464
Kāne'ohe, Hawai'i 96744
Email: info@beachhousepublishing.com
www.beachhousepublishing.com

Printed by RRD Dongguan, China 6/2021

Honu (Sea Turtle)

Spotted Pufferfish

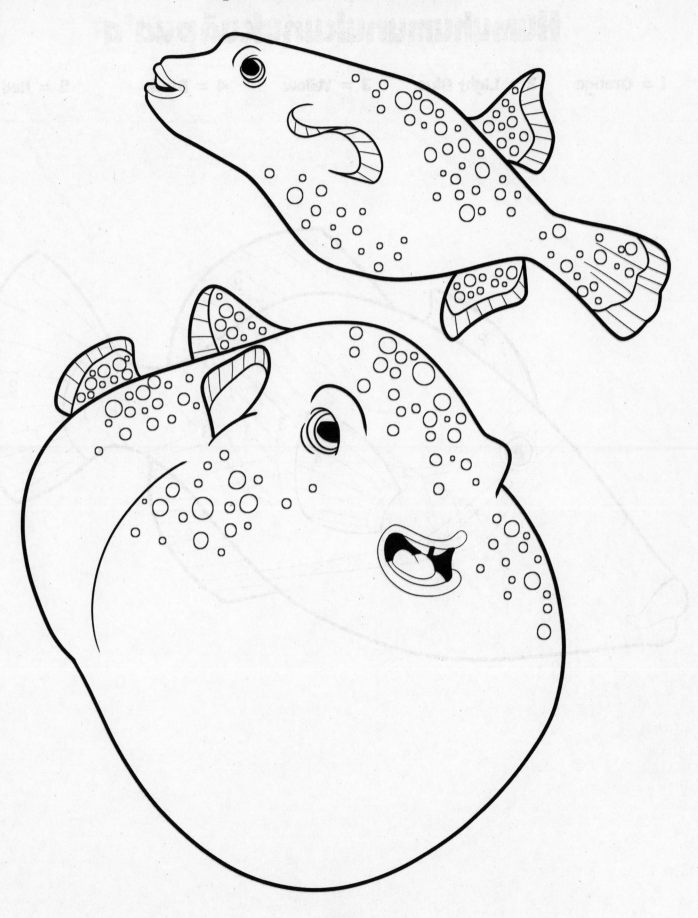

Color by Numbers
Humuhumunukunukuāpuaʻa

1 = Orange   2 = Light Blue   3 = Yellow   4 = Black   5 = Red

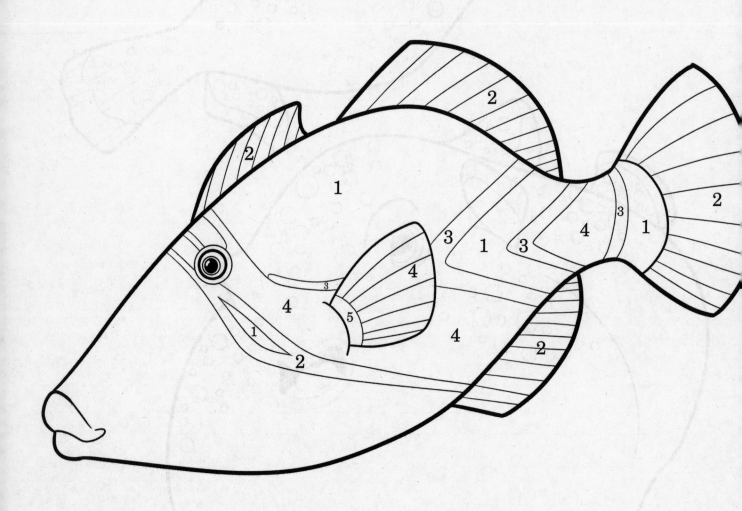

Longnose Butterflyfish

Blacktip Reef Shark

Blacktip Reef Shark

Which path should the baby honu take to reach the sea?

Connect the Dots
Monk Seal

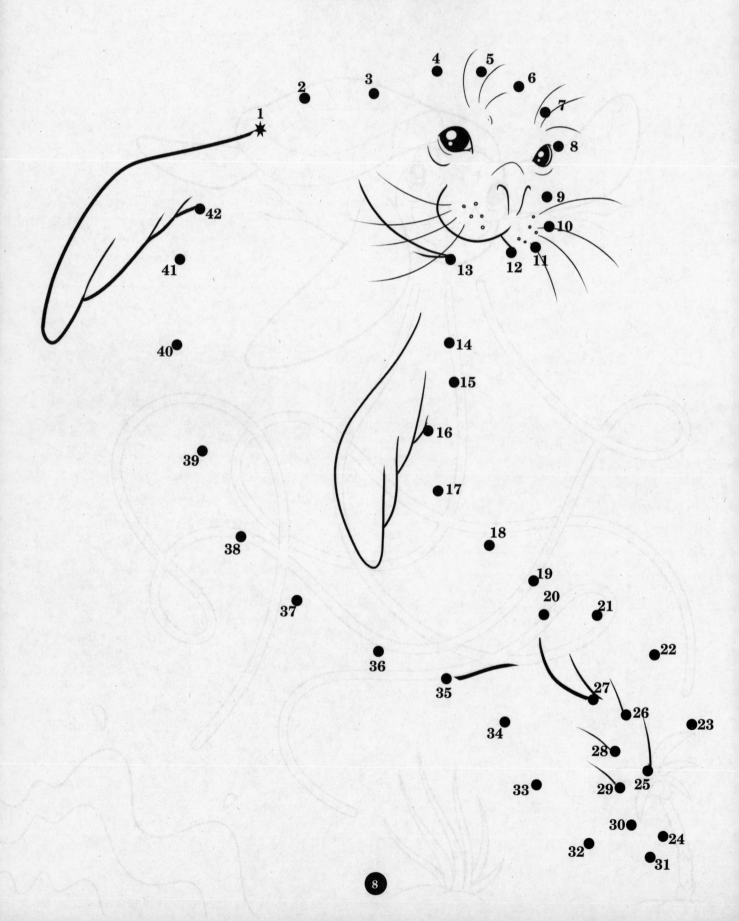

Flame Angelfish

Seahorse

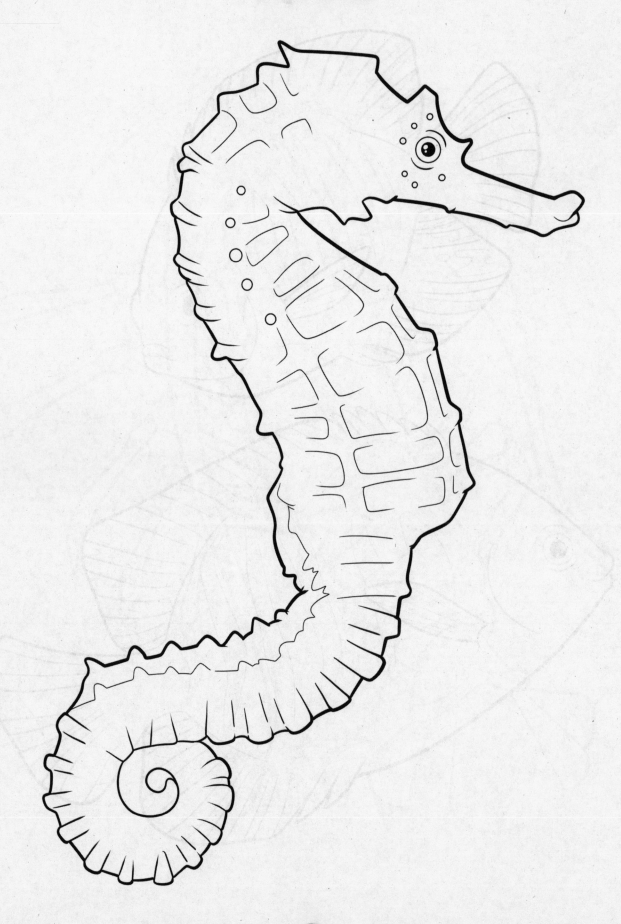

Dolphin

Match the animal to its name.

Monk Seal

Shark

Humpback Whale

Seahorse

Honu

Color by Numbers
Hawaiian Cleaner Wrasse

1 = Yellow   2 = Blue   3 = Purple   4 = Pink   5 = Black

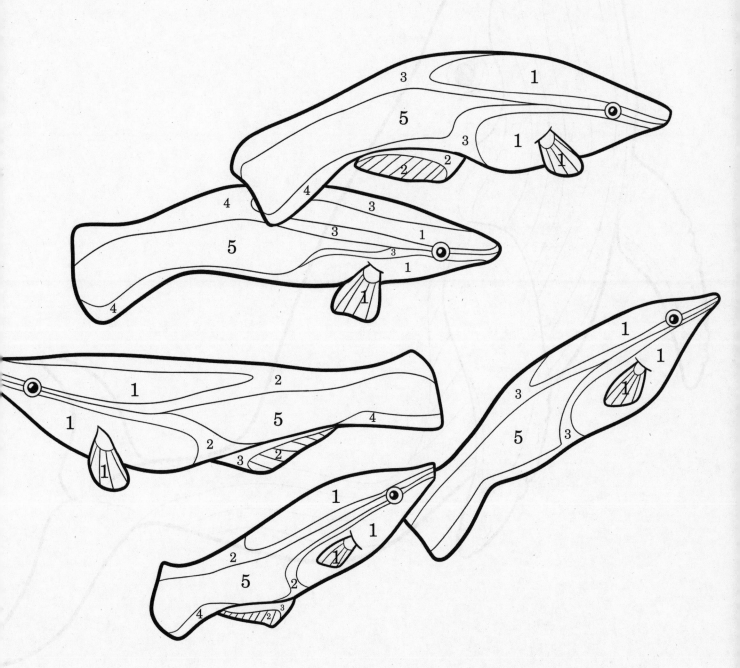

13

Humpback Whale

Humpback Whale

Hawaiian Spotted Eagle Ray

Circle the hermit crab that's different from the others.

Solve the picture code to learn the name of this fish.

E P S C H U I N F O R

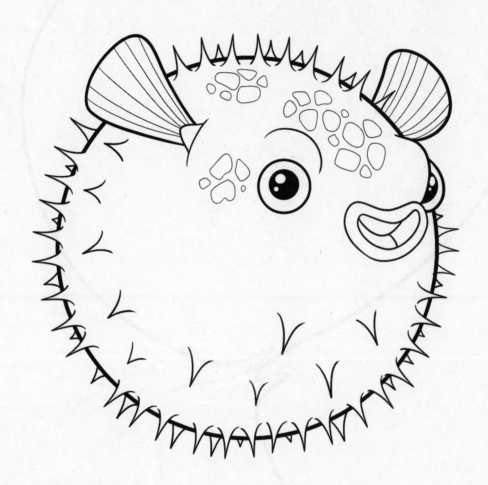

__ __ __ __ __ __ __ __ __ __ __ __ __

Manta Ray

Hawaiian Red Lionfish

Commerson's Frogfish

Parrotfish

Connect the Dots
Achilles Tang

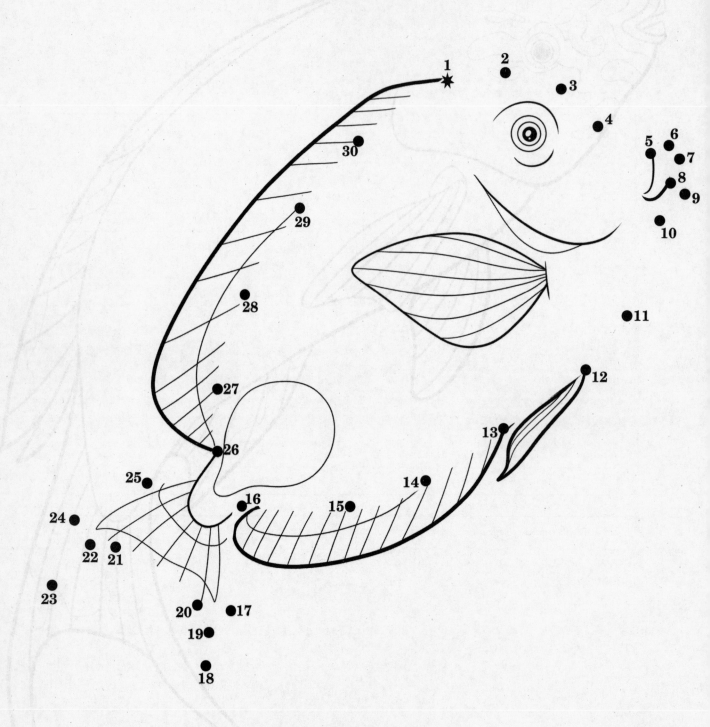

Go fishing for these fish!

```
W  S  Q  U  T  A  B  F
P  R  M  B  F  G  L  R
U  Z  A  H  I  O  E  O
F  L  N  S  T  A  N  G
F  A  I  H  S  A  N  F
E  I  N  M  H  E  Y  I
R  H  I  O  D  X  P  S
G  O  A  T  F  I  S  H
```

WRASSE

GOATFISH

TANG

MANINI

'AHI

FROGFISH

BLENNY

PUFFER

Unicornfish

Monk Seal

Color by Numbers
Surgeonfish Clean a Honu

1 = Yellow   2 = Green   3 = Dark Brown   4 = Light Brown   5 = Dark Green

Circle the 5 differences between these two pictures.

Sea Urchin and Achilles Tang

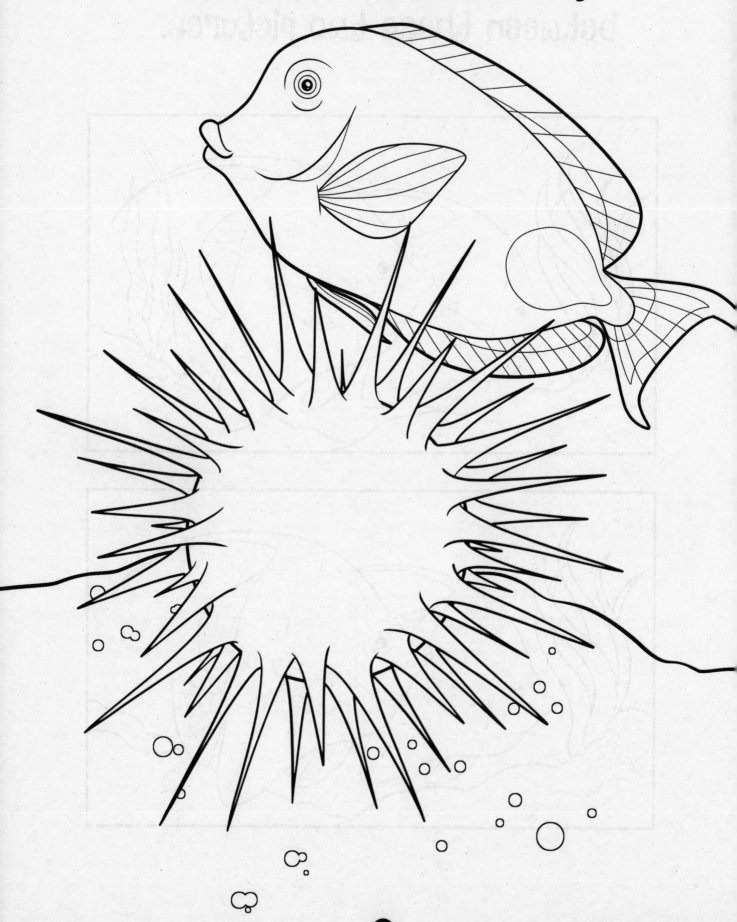

Giant Trevally

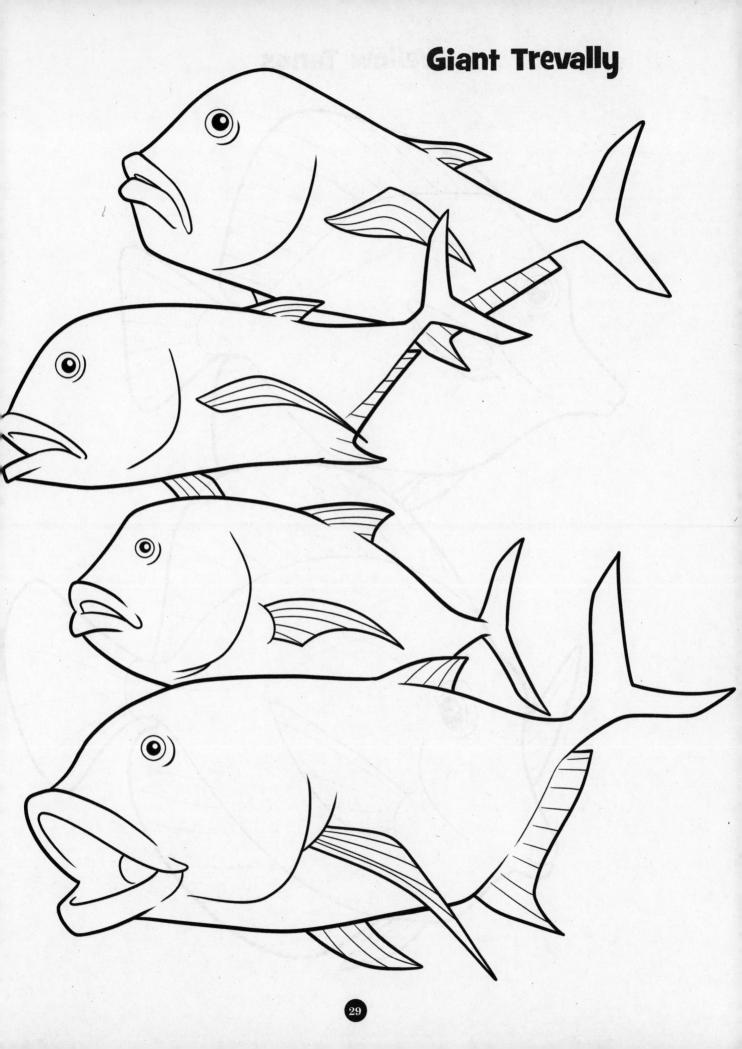

Yellow Tangs

Draw a line between each picture and its three close-ups.

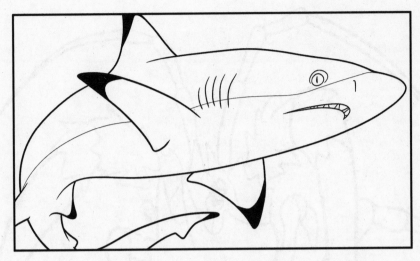

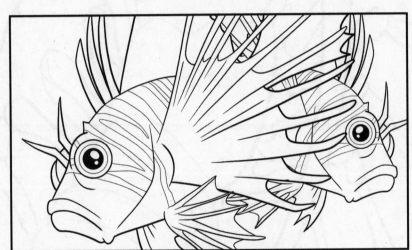

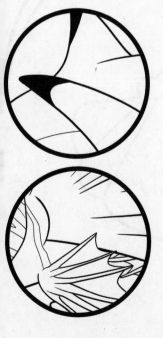
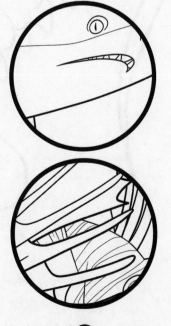
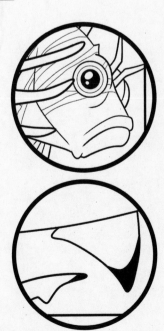

Spiny Lobster

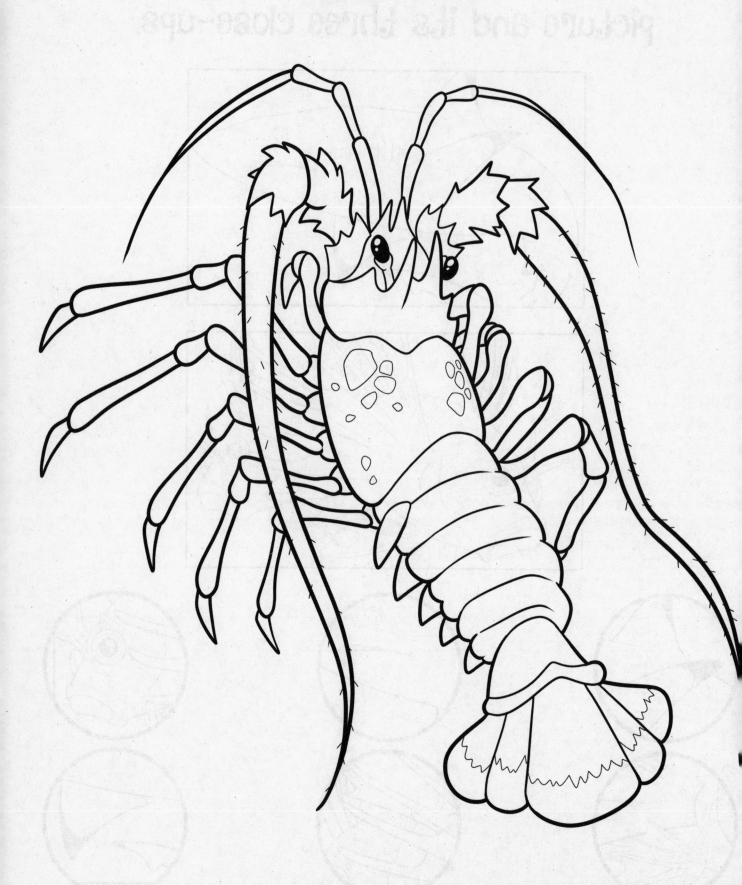

Color by Numbers
Snowflake Eel

1 = Yellow   2 = Black   3 = Gray

Sea Stars

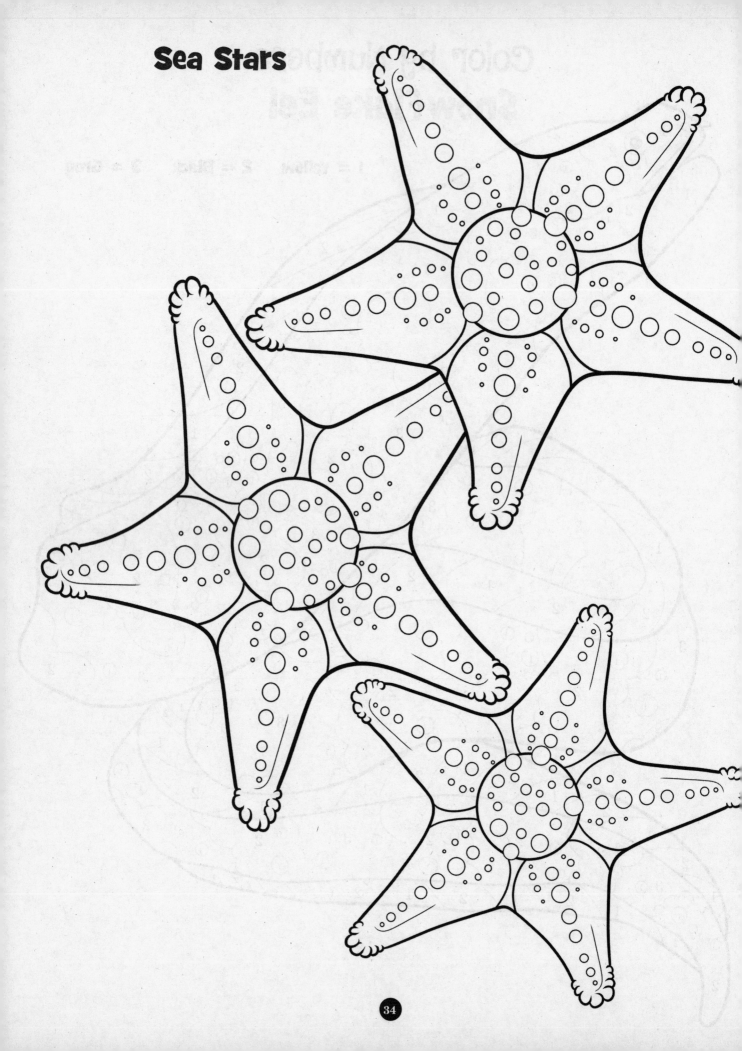

Octopus

Help the scuba diver find her way to the honu.

Pennant Butterflyfish

Ornate Butterflyfish

Connect the Dots
Hawaiian Spotted Eagle Ray

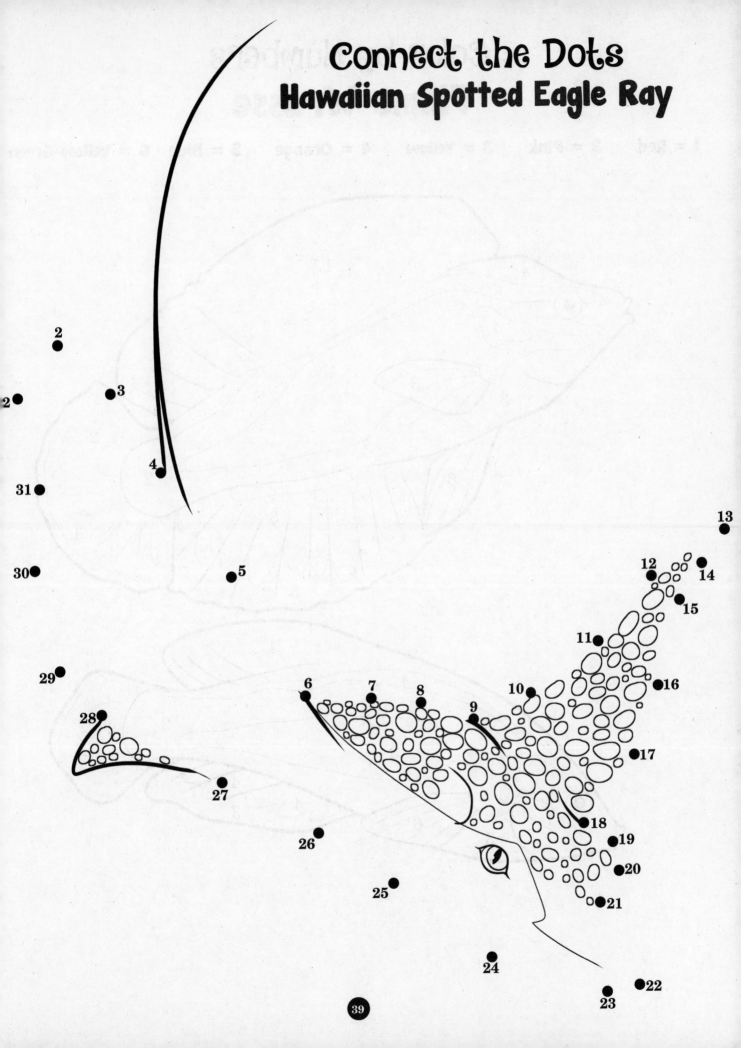

Color by Numbers
Flame Wrasse

1 = Red   2 = Pink   3 = Yellow   4 = Orange   5 = Blue   6 = Yellow-Green

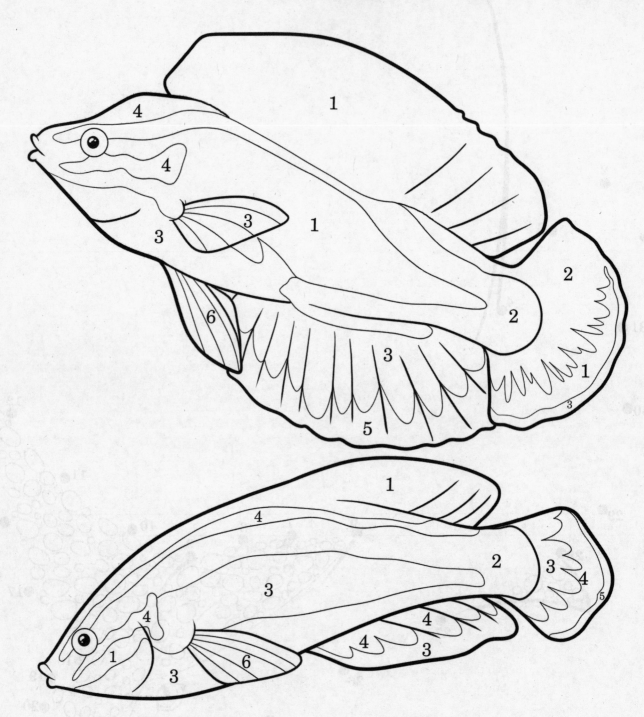

Hammerhead Shark

Hawaiian Fantail Filefish

Solve the picture code to reveal the monk seal's name in Hawaiian.

I   K   O   A   U   L   H

Answer: Ilioholoikauaua (loosely means "dog that runs in rough seas.")

43

Oriental Flying Gurnard

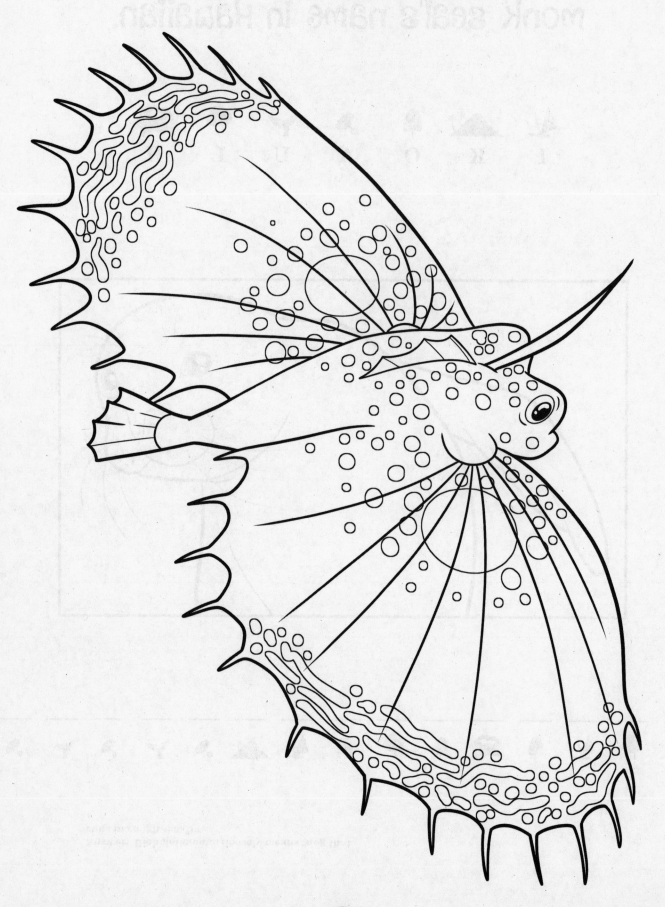

Hawaiian Squirrelfish

Draw a line between each picture and its three close-ups.

Moorish Idol

Broad Stingray

Broad Stingray

Circle the fish that's different from the others.

Bird Wrasse

Spinner Dolphins

Which path should the honu take to get cleaned by yellow tangs?

Flowery Flounder

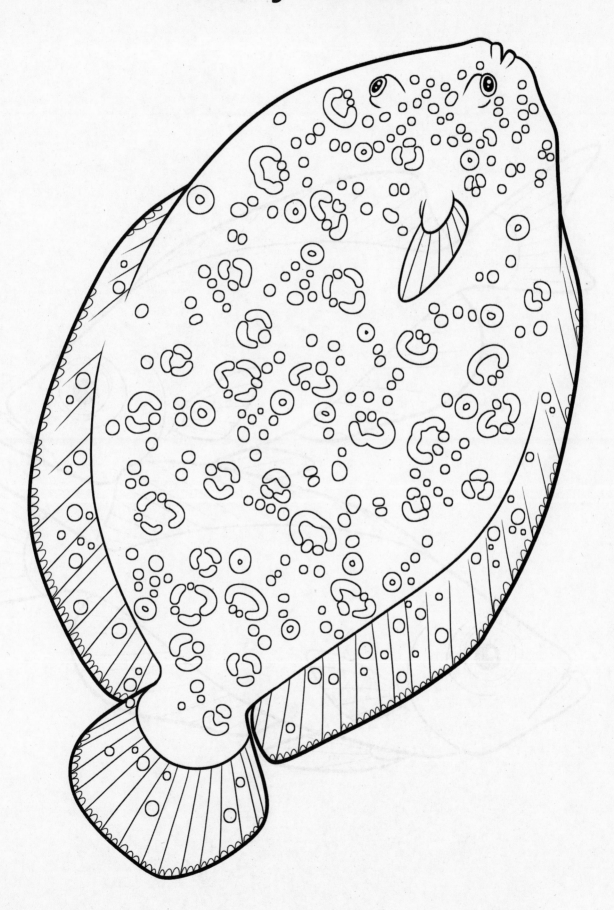

Hawaiian Big Eye

Milletseed Butterflyfish

Baby Honu

Lantern Toby

Circle the 5 differences between these two pictures.

Blacktip Reef Shark

Connect the Dots
Honu

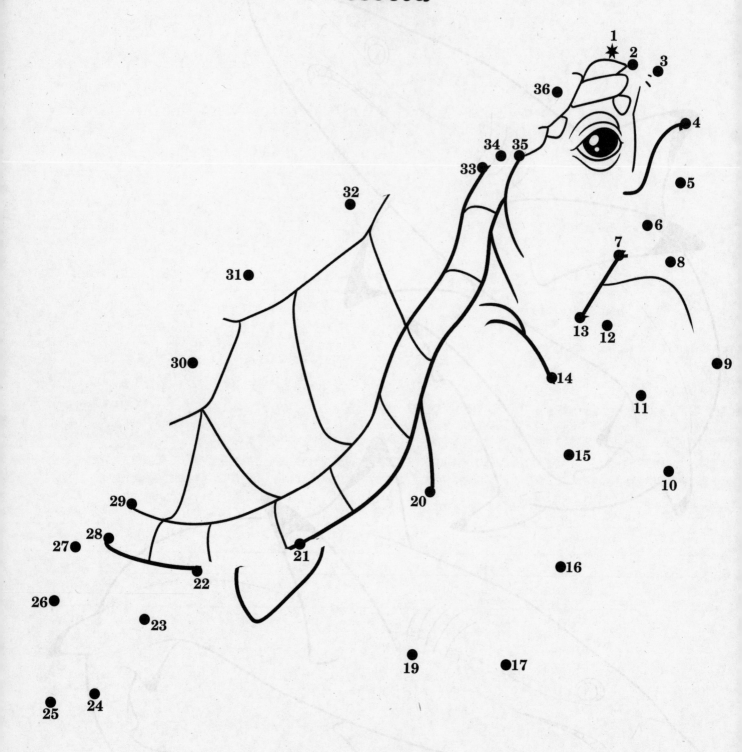

Monk Seal

Find these Hawai'i sea creatures!

```
M O N K S E A L
A C O R A L U E
N T M S H A R K
T O E H A I C D
A P N F I S H O
R U H A R K I C
A S A R D C N T
Y O N X S E M O
```

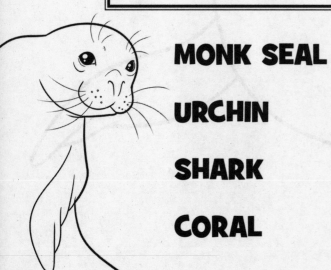

MONK SEAL　　　**MANTA RAY**

URCHIN　　　**OCTOPUS**

SHARK　　　**FISH**

CORAL

Answer

Color by Numbers
Sunset Wrasse

1 = Pink 2 = Bright Blue 3 = Orange 4 = Yellow 5 = Bright Green

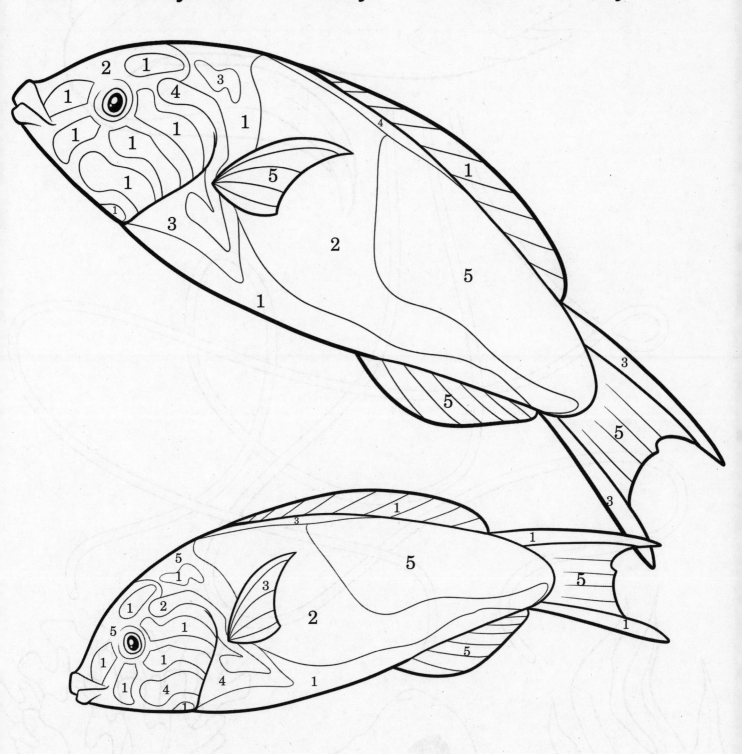

Help this eel find his cave!